SURPRISE
Storm

WRITTEN BY

Jessica Brody

ILLUSTRATED BY THE

Ameet Studio Artists

SUSTAINABLE
FORESTRY
INITIATIVE
Certified Sourcing
www.sfiprogram.org
SFI-01415

DISNEP PRESS

LOS ANGELES · NEW YORK

INTRODUCTION

Somewhere out there, in a bedroom much like yours, there was a girl who loved to build things with her LEGO bricks.

She had already built all the princess castles, so she decided to combine them and make a brand-new, super-special castle. Each day, she designed the castle a little differently, always changing it and imagining new ways for it to be magical.

In fact, it was the most magical, wonderful castle she had ever seen, but it was missing something—the princesses. Since this girl also loved the Disney Princesses, she put many of them into the castle, too.

Now the only thing left to do was make up story after story about her favorite princesses—and some new friends—having amazing adventures at the ever-changing castle.

This is one of those stories. . . .

CHAPTER 1

Princess Belle loved to read books. And her princess friends loved to listen to Belle reading books. One day, Belle's book was especially magical. And the princesses were especially interested.

When Belle got to a funny part, everyone laughed.

When she got to a suspenseful part, everyone leaned forward.

When she got to a scary part, everyone gasped.

Well, everyone except Rapunzel. She hid behind her long hair.

Belle was just getting to the really exciting part of the story when, suddenly, there was a loud knock on the castle door. Actually, it was more of a thump.

THUMP! THUMP! THUMP!

The princesses looked toward the door. Their faces were full of curiosity.

Who could it be? And who should answer the door?

Ariel really wanted to know who was there, so she went to answer.

At the same time, Jasmine, who felt like she was the leader, volunteered to see who was there.

And Mulan, being brave as usual, said she would do it.

CHAPTER 2

The princesses decided Mulan should open the door. She was the most courageous of them all. She was a warrior who knew how to fight in battles!

Mulan pulled the heavy castle door open a sliver and then smiled.

"It's the Mysterious Messenger!" she announced.

The princesses gathered around the front door to hear what the Mysterious Messenger had to say.

The Mysterious Messenger always brought fun and adventure. That day, however, she came with a warning. It sounded very serious.

"A glitter storm is coming!" the Mysterious Messenger announced.

The princesses looked at each other.

"A glitter storm!" repeated Rapunzel, hiding behind her hair again. "What should we do?"

The princesses turned back to the Mysterious Messenger to ask this very question. But the Mysterious Messenger had already mysteriously disappeared.

"Wow, she sure is mysterious," said Ariel.

"I know what we have to do,"
Jasmine said.

She was usually the first one to
take charge in a serious situation
like this. "We have to prepare the
castle. Close every window and every
door. Cover up all the flower beds.

Pull all the vehicles into the castle garage. Nothing should be left outside in the glitter."

The princesses leapt into action, running round the castle. They had to prepare for the incoming storm.

Now, it's important to remember that there were eight princesses who lived in this castle. That's a lot of princesses to keep track of. Which was probably why, in the confusion of the glitter storm, no one seemed to notice that one of the princesses was missing.

CHAPTER
3

A little ways away from the castle, across the stream in the nearby forest, Princess Aurora was having a very interesting conversation with a fox.

They were discussing the staircase Aurora was building.

You see, Aurora loved to climb to the tops of trees. She loved to sit in the branches.

Since she'd grown up in a forest, this was where she felt most at home.

Aurora wanted to invite her friends from the castle to join her in the tree, but she knew not all the princesses liked to climb trees. And Ariel was still a little too clumsy on her feet.

So Aurora had come up with the idea to build a staircase to the top of her favorite tree. That way her friends could enjoy the sunset with her.

"It should definitely be straight," Aurora said, stepping back a few paces. "It could start here and go up to that branch." She pointed at a sturdy branch above their heads.

The fox flicked his bushy tail. He curled it into a tight ball then let it loose again. He clearly disagreed.

"Hmm," Aurora replied. "You think it should go *around* the tree?"

The fox wiggled his ears.

"Interesting," said Aurora.

A very interesting conversation, indeed.

"I suppose that could work," Aurora decided.

She began gathering materials from the nearby wood. She placed the first step at the base of the tree. Then she stood back to admire her work. "Well, it's a start."

As Aurora continued to build her staircase, she had no idea that a short distance away, a thick cloud was hovering just above the castle, preparing to rain down buckets of glitter.

CHAPTER 4

Just outside the princesses' castle, there were lots of gardens. Some grew beautiful purple and pink flowers. Some grew gigantic fruit trees full of juicy apples—which everyone loved, except for Snow White.

But the most popular garden of them all was the vegetable garden.

It was very popular with the bunnies.

That day, most of the bunnies were hiding in their bunny holes because they had also heard the warning from the Mysterious Messenger. They knew about the glitter storm, and they didn't want to get their fur glittery.

But two of the bunnies hadn't heard
the warning.

Those bunnies did wonder, for a
moment, why they were the only
bunnies in the vegetable garden that day.

But they decided not to worry about it too much, because it meant they could eat as many carrots as they wanted.

Just as the bunnies were about to begin eating the carrots, the sky above their heads opened up. The cloud started to rain down heaps and heaps of glitter.

The bunnies looked at each other in surprise, then ran for the forest.

CHAPTER 5

Bunnies might be scared of glitter storms, but princesses are certainly not. The seven princesses who were inside the castle—Belle, Jasmine, Snow White, Rapunzel, Mulan, Cinderella, and Ariel—were watching in wonder from the window as glitter fell from the sky.

Ooh! thought Ariel. *This is so cool! It never rains glitter underwater.*

The glitter formed hills around the castle grounds.

"It reminds me of snow!" said Belle.

"Me?" asked Snow White.

Belle giggled. "Not *you*. Real snow."

"It reminds me of a sandstorm," said Jasmine, "but much more colorful."

"What does it remind you of, Aurora?" asked Mulan.

Everyone turned to see what Aurora's answer would be. Mulan looked at Belle.

Belle looked at Jasmine.

Jasmine looked at Ariel.

Ariel looked at Rapunzel.

Rapunzel looked at Snow White.

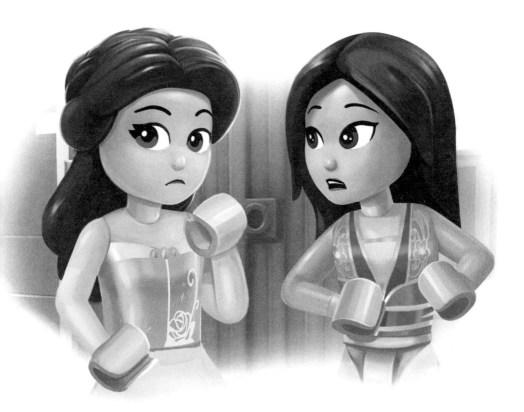

Snow White looked at Cinderella.

But no one looked at Aurora.

Because Aurora wasn't there.

"Where's Aurora?" Ariel asked, a little panicked.

No one knew.

"She must be walking in the forest,"
Cinderella guessed. She looked out
the window. The storm seemed to be
directly above the castle. And nowhere
else.

"Did anyone close the window in her room?" Jasmine asked.

Cinderella looked at Snow White.

Snow White looked at Rapunzel.

Rapunzel looked at Ariel.

Ariel looked at Jasmine.

Jasmine looked at Belle.

Belle looked at Mulan.

But it was clear that no one had closed the window.

Which meant that the window had been open during the whole storm.

Oops!

CHAPTER 6

As soon as the storm was over, all the princesses raced up the castle stairs and down the hallway. Finally, they reached Aurora's forest-themed bedroom.

"Poisoned apples!" Snow White gasped.

"Jumping jellyfish!" Ariel cried.

"This is bad," said Rapunzel.

Jasmine cleared her throat. "No, no. It's okay. It's not bad."

But Rapunzel was right. It *was* kind of bad. The glitter storm had torn the room apart.

The chair and nightstand were in pieces. And there was glitter *everywhere*.

"Look!" cried Ariel. "Her whatchamacallit is gone!" Ariel sometimes had trouble remembering the human names for things.

"It's called a canopy bed," Belle gently reminded Ariel.

"Where will she sleep?" Rapunzel asked.

"Calm down," Jasmine said, taking control again.

"We'll just have to fix everything before she gets back."

"Good idea!" Snow White sang as she twirled. "I can get my birds to help clear the glitter."

"And I'll get the mice to help, too!" said Cinderella.

"I can rebuild the chair!" Mulan offered.

"And I can rebuild the nightstand!" said Ariel.

"And Belle and I will head to the castle workshop to build Aurora a new bed," said Jasmine.

"But will there be enough time?" Cinderella said. "What if she comes back before we're finished?"

"I'll go look for her in the forest and distract her!" Rapunzel said. "I know a shortcut across the bridge."

"Good," Jasmine said, happy to see all her friends pitching in. She clapped her hands. "Everyone has a job to do. Now let's do it!"

CHAPTER

7

Aurora and the fox had just finished building the staircase for her favorite tree when, suddenly, two bunnies covered in glitter burst into the forest.

"Goodness!" Aurora said, kneeling down to look at them. "You two look terrified. What happened?"

The first bunny wiggled his nose. The
other bunny thumped her foot. Then
the first bunny scratched his ear, while
the second bunny—

"Whoa, whoa," Aurora said. "Slow
down. One at a time." She pointed
to the first bunny, who explained the
situation.

"A glitter storm?" Aurora said,
surprised. "At the castle?"

The two bunnies nodded.

Aurora jumped to her feet. "I have to go check on my friends to make sure they're okay!" She beckoned for the fox and the bunnies to follow her. "Come on! I know a shortcut through the meadow!"

Aurora started to run toward the meadow, which, by the way, was nowhere near the bridge.

And that was why, when Rapunzel reached the forest a few minutes later, Aurora was nowhere to be found.

CHAPTER 8

Jasmine and Belle were in a race against time. They had to get to the castle workshop to build a new bed before Aurora got back.

The problem with huge castles is that there are several ways to get places. Jasmine was convinced she knew the fastest way to get to the castle workshop.

She wanted to go through her magic
courtyard. That would take them
around Mulan's training center, up the
stairs of Cinderella's balcony, and past
the dining room.

But Belle was convinced that it was
faster to go through Ariel's grotto,
around Snow White's wishing well,
up the stairs of Rapunzel's tower, and
through Belle's library.

In truth, the routes were exactly the same distance. Jasmine just really liked to go through her magic courtyard, and Belle just really liked to go through her library.

They decided the best way to choose which way to go was to play their favorite game: jewel-cloth-sword.

The two princesses faced each other, ready to go.

"One, two, three!" Jasmine counted.

They called out the word "jewel" at the same time.

"One, two, three!" Belle counted.

They both called out "sword" at the same time. Another tie.

Jasmine huffed. "Stop choosing the same one as me!"

"Stop choosing the same one as *me*!" said Belle.

"One more time," said Jasmine. "One, two, three!"

Belle shouted "jewel" as Jasmine yelled out "cloth." Cloth covered jewel. Jasmine won.

"C'mon!" said Jasmine, pointing toward her magic courtyard. "This way!"

The two princesses set off. They ran through the courtyard, then curved around Mulan's training center. Next they bounded up the steps of Cinderella's balcony and darted past the dining room. Finally, they came to the long hallway that led to the workshop.

They ran down the hallway only to find . . .

The workshop was gone!

CHAPTER 9

Rapunzel searched the forest. She looked inside logs. She looked under beds of leaves. She even looked up in the trees! But Aurora was still nowhere to be found.

"Where could she be?" she asked, but there was no one there to answer.

Then Rapunzel spotted two
chipmunks peeking out from behind a
tree, and she got an idea.

Aurora was always hanging out with
animals in the forest. Maybe *they* knew
where to find her.

"Hello," Rapunzel called out to the chipmunks. "Have you seen—"

But the chipmunks had just heard about a pile of carrots that had been left in the middle of the vegetable garden.

And they couldn't pass up a free feast.

So they ran away before Rapunzel could finish her question.

CHAPTER 10

"**W**here is the workshop?" Jasmine asked as she and Belle stared at the wall where the door used to be.

"I don't know!" replied Belle. "This castle is *always* changing."

"I know," said Jasmine. "Just yesterday, I found a balcony outside of my room!"

"And two days ago I noticed a new tower across from Ariel's room," Belle remarked.

"The workshop must have moved," said Jasmine. "Think! Have you seen any extra doors lately?"

They both sat down to think. But as Belle leaned against the wall, a door behind her opened. She fell backward.

"Hmm," Belle said thoughtfully as she lay on the floor in the doorway. "I don't remember that door being there a minute ago."

"It wasn't," Jasmine said. "But look!"

She stepped over Belle into the room that had magically just appeared.

Belle sat up and turned around. She gasped when she saw where they were. She couldn't have been more delighted by what she saw. "It's the workshop!" she cried out, beaming at Jasmine.

CHAPTER 11

The castle workshop was even better than Belle and Jasmine had remembered. There was everything a princess could ever dream of building with: wood, metal, fabric, lace, ribbons, sparkles, string, flowers, and even jewels!

"This is amazing!" Belle said.

"Quick!" Jasmine told her. "Let's get to work. We're running out of time!"

The two princesses went to work building a new bed for Aurora.

They put pieces together to make the bed. Then they decorated it with a few flowers to make it pretty. But it didn't take long for Belle to realize they were running out of pieces.

"Oh, no!" cried Belle. "We won't have enough to finish the bed!"

Just then, they heard someone singing.

Jasmine ran to the window and saw Aurora wandering out of the meadow. "She's back!"

CHAPTER 12

Aurora sang as she walked up the path to the castle. The fox and bunnies who were following her tried to sing, too. But they were off-key, in a cute way. As she neared the magical castle, Aurora immediately noticed that the castle grounds were covered in glitter!

She also noticed how quiet everything was. Normally, there were princesses everywhere. Mulan was usually practicing her sword fighting in her training center.

Ariel was usually frolicking in the castle moat. Belle was usually curled up under a tree with a book. But there was no one around.

"Hmm," Aurora said. "I wonder where everyone is."

She took another step toward the castle, but her foot caught on something, and suddenly she was falling. She landed in a pile of glitter with an *oof.* She looked back to see what she'd tripped over.

At first Aurora thought it was a rope. But then she saw the mysterious thing sparkle in the sunlight, and she knew it wasn't a rope.

"Rapunzel?" she called out curiously, glancing around. "I know you're here. I just tripped over your hair."

"Oh!" Rapunzel suddenly appeared from behind a bush.

"Oops! Sorry about that," she said,
winking at Aurora. "I should keep better
track of this stuff." She scooped up her
magical hair. Her plan to stall Aurora
had finally worked!

But then Aurora stood up and
continued to walk toward the castle.
Rapunzel ran ahead and jumped in
front of her. "Hey!" she said. "Let's go
for a walk!"

"But I just went for a walk," said
Aurora.

"Let's go for another walk! I know
how much you love the forest!"

Aurora was confused. Rapunzel was
acting strange. "I think I'm going to go
to my room and take a nap."

"NO!" Rapunzel cried, jumping in
front of her once again. She knew she
absolutely could not let Aurora go to her
room. Not yet. It wouldn't be ready!

"Why not?" Aurora asked.

"Because . . . because . . ." Rapunzel
tried to think of an excuse. But she
couldn't. She sighed and let Aurora
pass.

Rapunzel watched in disappointment as Aurora walked up the steps and opened the castle door. A few moments later, Rapunzel heard Aurora gasp and cry out, "What happened to my room?!"

CHAPTER
13

Nothing had gone according to plan. Aurora's room didn't look anything like it had before. And Jasmine was frustrated that no one had followed her directions.

The mice and birds hadn't *cleaned up* the glitter. They'd spread it around to decorate the room.

Ariel hadn't rebuilt the nightstand—she'd turned it into a fish tank. It had shells and fish from the moat inside of it.

The chair that Mulan had reconstructed was the wrong shape. It looked more like a couch than a chair, with extra-wide arms.

And the bed was still only half built.

But Jasmine had no time to fix anything, because just then, Aurora walked in and cried out, "What happened to my room?!"

"I'm so sorry," Jasmine apologized. "We tried to make it look exactly the same, but—"

"I LOVE IT!" Aurora said, interrupting her. "I've always wanted a fish tank.

"And that chair was always too small.

"And the glitter makes everything so sparkly!"

She grinned as she looked around the room, taking everything in.

"So, you like it?" Jasmine asked, confused.

"Yes! Thank you! This is so much better! And is that a new bed?!"

Belle looked at the half-finished bed. "Yes. But we ran out of decorations."

Aurora winked at Belle and held up
her basket. The princesses could now
see it was filled with flowers and twigs
and leaves that Aurora had collected
from the forest.

They had all the materials they
needed!

CHAPTER
14

All the princesses pitched in, and together, they finished building Aurora's bed.

"It's a dream bed," Rapunzel proclaimed.

"It's beautiful," added Cinderella.

"Now all we need is a good story!" Aurora said.

"I can handle that!" Belle told her. She pulled out her book and got comfy on the new chair. Now that it was bigger, Mulan and Ariel could sit next to her.

The rest of the princesses gathered around, and Belle started to read. After a few minutes, they heard quiet snoring and looked over to see that Aurora had fallen asleep on her new bed.

It had been a very exciting day, after all.

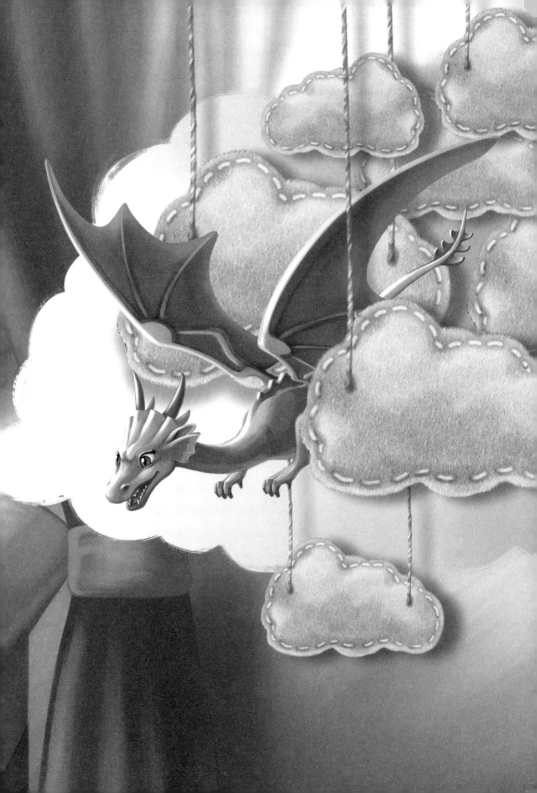

Cinderella

Jasmine

Mulan

BELLE

SNOW WHITE

ARIEL

AURORA

RAPUNZEL

LEGO Disney PRINCESS

First Paperback Edition, October 2018
1 3 5 7 9 10 8 6 4 2
ISBN 978-1-368-02414-3
FAC-029261-18257

Library of Congress Control Number: 2018936688

Designed by Margie Peng

Printed in the United States of America

For more Disney Press fun, visit www.disneybooks.com